Prospect Heights Public Library

P9-CLV-243

Not
FOR SALE

JUL 15

ORCA
Echoes

Not
FOR SALE

Sara Cassidy

illustrated by Helen Flook

Prospect Heights Public Library
12 N. Elm Street
Prospect Heights, IL 60070
www.phpl.info

ORCA BOOK PUBLISHERS

Text copyright © 2015 Sara Cassidy
Illustrations copyright © 2015 Helen Flook

All rights reserved. No part of this publication may be reproduced or transmitted in
any form or by any means, electronic or mechanical, including photocopying,
recording or by any information storage and retrieval system now known or to be
invented, without permission in writing from the publisher.

Library and Archives Canada Cataloguing in Publication

Cassidy, Sara, author
Not for sale / Sara Cassidy; illustrator: Helen Flook.
(Orca echoes)

Issued in print and electronic formats.
ISBN 978-1-4598-0719-8 (pbk.).—ISBN 978-1-4598-0720-4 (pdf).—
ISBN 978-1-4598-0721-1 (epub)

I. Flook, Helen, illustrator II. Title. III. Series: Orca echoes
PS8555.A7812N67 2015   jc813'.54   C2014-906691-0
C2014-906692-9

First published in the United States, 2015
Library of Congress Control Number: 2014952070

Summary: When Cyrus's adoptive parents tell him they are selling their house, he devises a
plan to sabotage the move.

Orca Book Publishers gratefully acknowledges the support for its publishing programs
provided by the following agencies: the Government of Canada through the Canada Book Fund
and the Canada Council for the Arts, and the Province of British Columbia
through the BC Arts Council and the Book Publishing Tax Credit.

*Orca Book Publishers is dedicated to preserving the environment and
has printed this book on Forest Stewardship Council® certified paper.*

Cover artwork and interior illustrations by Helen Flook
Author photo by Amaya Tarasoff

ORCA BOOK PUBLISHERS   ORCA BOOK PUBLISHERS
PO Box 5626, STN. B   PO Box 468
Victoria, BC Canada   Custer, WA USA
V8R 6S4   98240-0468

www.orcabook.com
Printed and bound in Canada.

18 17 16 15 • 4 3 2 1

For Ezra

Chapter One

Ancient potatoes lurk in our bedroom closets. Under beds with dust bunnies. In the toes of rubber boots no one has worn since spring. When Mom finds one of the withered gray tubers, she waves it in our faces.

"Do your homework, Rudy!" she says. "Cyrus, clean your room! Or I'll touch you with this putrid thing. I'll cook it in your soup without you knowing!"

A slimy tornado of fear whirls in my throat at the thought of wrinkly-potato soup. I try not to gag.

I expect the potato to clink and clack when Mom shakes it in my face, but of course it doesn't. It's not a baby's rattle, it's a potato. A potato that looks like it's had a fight with a hole punch. The shriveled spud is

1

the leftover ammo from a potato-gun battle between my brother Rudy and me. Rudy's eight, and I'm nine.

A potato gun looks like a water pistol, but instead of water, you fill it with potato. First, you find a big potato in the stinky kitchen drawer. Then you shove the gun's short barrel in past the peel to load it with potato flesh. A potato pellet is shaped like a pencil eraser, only it's crunchy and white, not rubbery and pink.

It doesn't exactly hurt when you get shot with a potato pellet, but it can sting. Sometimes, if Mom's out of potatoes, Rudy and I battle with apples. Once, when Mom was at work, we tried a banana. It was disgusting. Banana pellets don't sting—they just mush and dribble.

Eventually, Rudy and I tire of shooting each other with bits of spud. We get distracted by the TV or LEGO. Or by Wigglechin, our cat, who is old and often clinging to things she's trying not to fall from. Like the living room curtains or the dining-room chandelier.

We drop our guns and leave our hole-pocked potatoes to fester where they fall. A month or two later, Mom discovers one and shakes it at us. I sure wish I wasn't so frightened of a withered potato. ·

Chapter Two

Rudy is not my brother's full name. I'm not allowed to say his full name because it upsets him. But sometimes, late at night, I crawl deep under my covers and say it very softly. Just to hear it out loud.

You can probably figure out what it is. Think what Rudy might be short for. Want a clue? Red-nosed reindeer.

Got it?

But why would my mother pick a name that no one is allowed to say?

Mom says when Rudy was born, he came out howling like a wolf. Guess what R___ means? *Brave wolf*. So even though a magical Christmas reindeer is the first thing people think of when they hear that name, Mom felt it was meant to be.

Rudy? A brave wolf? More like a scaredy-cat. Rudy gets stomachaches when it's time to go to school. If we're heading to a party, he hides under his blankets. When a waiter asks for his order, he goes mute. When Rudy gets anxious, Mom reminds him to take long, deep breaths. In through the nose, out through the mouth.

Most of the time, though, Rudy is lots of fun. He and I love to perch in high places. We play marbles up on closet shelves, eat our snacks squatting on the mantelpiece or even on top of the fridge. I once saw Rudy sit on a *door*, while it was open, and read up there. I don't know how he did it. I would try, but it looks very uncomfortable.

Mom thinks our desire to be up high comes from our great-grandmother, who was a trapeze artist. "That's the most dangerous occupation in the world," Mom always says. "The second most dangerous job is West Coast logger."

We go silent when Mom says that, because Dad is a West Coast logger. He's often away in the woods, where he operates a feller buncher. A feller buncher is a big vehicle that cuts down—or fells—trees, then gathers them in a bunch. Dad lives in a logging camp with other big, strong, hungry people like him. Loggers eat a lot. There's a place in camp called the *dessert shack*. It's a shed that's open all day and night, and it's filled with pies, cakes, brownies, Jell-O— anything you want. Hot chocolate too. But Dad still misses us. He says he'd choose us over hot chocolate any day. I'm glad Dad eats a lot and is so big. That way, if a tree falls on him, he won't be smushed.

"Yes, your great-grandma liked being up high," Mom tells us. "It was in her genes, and now it's in yours. Maybe you'll end up building skyscrapers or being astronauts or champion bungee jumpers."

"I miss Great-Grandma," Rudy sniffs.

"I know, honey," Mom says.

"You never even met Great-Grandma!" I say.

"So?"

"He wishes he had," Mom says.

"Yeah," Rudy blubbers.

That's Rudy for you.

We're eating supper. It's our first time having what Mom calls "Q salad." It's made with quinoa and kumquat. Every time Mom runs to the kitchen to get more napkins or milk, Rudy dumps a handful from his plate onto mine. Now I've got twice as much as he has. I haven't tried any yet. Rudy keeps crossing his eyes and sticking his finger down his throat to show me how delicious it is.

Finally, I take a bite. Q salad is delicious! It's sweet and nutty. Rudy stares as I load up spoonful after spoonful. He makes a face at me like I've got a problem, but I can tell he's kind of jealous. I think it's hard for him not liking many foods.

Mom puts her fork down. She looks at me, then at Rudy. "Kids," she says. "I've got serious news. I want you to listen carefully and not freak out."

Rudy drops his fork and leaps onto the counter.

"We've got to move," Mom announces. "This house is too big for us."

"But I'm growing," I say.

"Me too," says Rudy. "And Dad's huge."

"I know," Mom says. "And that's great. But I've got fewer hours of work, so I'm making less money, and Dad has less work too, because the forest needs a chance to grow right now. We can't afford to heat this big house anymore."

"Could we have a lemonade stand?" I offer.

"I'll give you my paper-route money," Rudy says.

"Thanks, sweethearts," Mom says. "I've thought of all that, but it won't be enough. We'll be cozier in a small house. We'll play lots of board games. Okay?"

Rudy looks terrified.

"Breathe, Rudy," Mom says. "We'll still have a roof over our heads, and our stuff will come with us. Just the floors and walls will be different."

"And the view outside my window." Rudy pouts.

"The new view could be better," Mom says.

"Yeah," I say. "Besides, what's your view now? Old Jacob in his kitchen, putting his teeth in?"

It's true. Rudy's bedroom window looks right into Old Jacob's place next door. One day, we watched as he shoved his false teeth into his mouth with one hand, then a piece of buttered toast with the other. I imitate Old Jacob's teeth-and-toast routine. Rudy laughs and the fear seems to drain from his face.

Something streaks past the window, like a clump of snow sliding off the roof in winter. I run to the window in time to see Wigglechin squirming in the tulip bed below. She has probably been dangling from the rain gutter for the past hour. She struggles to stand, then tiptoes away with her nose in the air as if nothing happened. Her fur is caked with dirt.

Chapter Three

I may have made Rudy laugh about Old Jacob. But the whole time, my heart was falling through my rib cage faster than Wigglechin shot past the kitchen window.

Our house holds me the way my body holds me. I've lived at 637 Petunia Boulevard ever since I came to live with Mom and Dad. I was two months old when we first met. I don't know much about my life before then. Who remembers the first two months of their life? I could have been at the top of a volcano in a wet diaper or falling through space from another planet.

Mom says I was looked after those first two months by Kimmy, my birth mom. Mom says Kimmy loved me very much, but she was too young to look after me. If I ever want to meet her, Mom says I can. Maybe one day I will.

I pull a chair up to the fish tank and watch Einstein swim back and forth. We named him Einstein because his head is really big. We pretend he's super intelligent.

"We're moving," I whisper to him. "Isn't that the stupidest thing you ever heard?"

Einstein stops swimming. He looks right at me. I nod. He waggles his head back and forth. He usually does this when he's hungry, but I think he can't believe we're moving either. Still, I give him a pinch of food. He swims to the top for the flecks, but I swear he moves more slowly than usual.

"You're lucky," I say. I tap lightly on the side of Einstein's aquarium. "You get to take your house with you."

I climb up on the piano and try to read for a while before bed, but I keep losing my place on the page.

I read the same sentence over four times, and I still don't know what it says. I'm thinking about where we're moving to, but I can't picture anything. I look around at our house and see it as I've never seen it before. I mean, I see the walls and the ceilings and the floors. But for the first time ever, they're apart from me. It's like they've loosened their grip.

Chapter Four

There's a new kid in my gymnastics class. His hair sticks up and he never stops hopping from one foot to the other like he has to pee.

"This is Rudy," says Coach Alex, who's from Russia. "Please welcome him warmly."

"I know your real name," I whisper to "Rudy" when we're in line for the tumble track.

"Yeah," the boy says, slightly out of breath from jumping foot to foot. "Rudy."

"I mean your *full* name." I raise my eyebrows.

The boy slows his bouncing. "Rudy Walker?"

"*Come on,*" I say. The boy stops bouncing and

looks at me as if I'm crazy. "My brother has the same name. I know all about it."

"Your brother's name is Rudy Walker?"

"It's more than that. You know it."

"Well, with my middle name, it's Rudy James Walker."

"Nothing else?"

"Nothing else."

"Hmm."

"I'll prove it. Okay?"

"Rudy!" the coach calls. "Tumble."

Rudy runs down the tumble track, stopping to somersault every few steps. Then he hurls himself off the end of the track into the foam pit. The foam pit is like an aquarium. Only instead of water, it's filled with giant blocks of foam. Finally, it's my turn to run. I pretend I'm a bowling ball rolling down the alley. I imagine five bowling pins planted in the air above the foam pit, like phantoms with little heads and wide hips. I knock them all down.

"I'll bring my birth certificate next week," Rudy tells me when we're back in line. "You'll see."

I start humming the Christmas song under my breath. But I've got to say, the kid is pretty good at pretending he has no idea what I'm talking about.

When I get home from gymnastics, I get a shock. A For Sale sign is plunged into our front yard. On the sign is a photo of a smiling woman. *Moving? Let Marsha Plannet Help You Plan It!* Marsha Plannet has big white teeth and Playmobil hair. As if all the hairs are fused into one solid lump.

"Who's she?" I ask Mom.

"She's our real-estate agent."

"She's real?"

"Well, sometimes people overwork their photos. They photoshop out the wrinkles and the blotches and whatnot."

"You mean she's actually wrinkly and blotchy?"

"She's real, that's all I'm saying."

"I hate her."

"You haven't even met her."

"So once I meet her, *then* I can hate her?"

"*Cyrus.*"

Rudy is in his room, playing with LEGO. His curtains are drawn.

"I don't want to see that stupid sign," he mutters.

I peek through the curtains. "You might want to see it now."

I point to Wigglechin, who is dangling by her paws from the bottom of the sign. Rudy and I laugh, but then I notice something. As Wigglechin struggles, the For Sale sign wobbles back and forth.

That's when I get my awesome idea.

Chapter Five

Mom is on her knees scrubbing the hall floor. She reaches under the black dresser and pulls out a shriveled potato. "Add it to the pile, will you?"

I don't move. I'm sitting up high, on a windowsill. Mom throws the withered ball at my head.

"Ow!"

Mom has been cleaning the house for three days. She's also been paying Rudy and me nickels to lug boxes of thrift-shop donations to the lawn. She's getting the house ready for "buyers."

"You need to get your hair cut," she tells me.

"That will help sell the house?"

"Maybe. But also, Dad's coming home tomorrow."

We always get our hair cut before Dad comes home. We take long baths with hot water, fresh bars of soap and fluffy facecloths too. I think Mom wants it to look like she's been taking extra good care of us.

"Rudy!" I call. "Dad's coming home. We're going to Burt's."

"No!" Rudy dives into his closet.

"Come on. We'll get a lollipop!"

Burt the barber always gives us a lollipop after he has brushed the backs of our necks with his tickly miniature broom. I check my lollipop carefully for hairs before licking.

"I don't care." Rudy pouts.

Mom rolls her eyes. "Rudy, you need to take ten deep breaths. Come on now. Dad will want to see you with a nice fresh haircut."

"You gave away my push doggie."

"Rudy, you haven't played with Push-Push since you were four."

"And you gave away my Pokemon cards!"

"I won't donate any more of your toys unless you okay it."

"Promise?"

"If you get your hair cut."

So Rudy and I walk to Burt's and get our necks tickled and a lollipop each. Walking home, the back of Rudy's neck looks so naked I want to wrap a scarf around it. My earlobes feel every breeze. It's nice, though, being freshly trimmed for Dad. I feel brand-new. Like the world is starting over. But there's something frightening in the breeze too. It's like the sidewalk could disappear in front of me. One step and I'd be falling through space.

At home, we climb into the cherry tree to eat our lollipops. While we're perched in the branches, the thrift-shop truck pulls up and two women remove the boxes of donations from the lawn. They don't notice Rudy and me dangling our feet above them. When they leave, there's just one stupid thing left in the yard—the stupid For Sale sign with the stupid photo of stupid Martian Planet.

But hey, Dad will be home tomorrow. And he snores really loudly. Loud snores are just what I need if I'm going to stop us from losing this house.

Chapter Six

Not only do we get new haircuts, but Mom comes home with a brand-new pair of jeans for each of us. They're the stiffest, darkest jeans I've ever seen. Mine are huge. I have to cinch up the waist until they're all puckered. I rub against the trunk of the cherry tree, hoping to fade them.

Mom leans out a window. "What are you doing to that tree?"

I look down at my jeans. They're as dark as ever. I look at the tree. The trunk is worn smooth.

"Just an experiment," I mumble.

"Some buyers are coming to look at the house. Could you please clean Einstein's aquarium?"

"Why doesn't Rudy have to do it?"

"You know how Rudy feels about cold water."

I remember Rudy up to his waist in various lakes and swimming pools, bawling his eyes out.

"I don't like cold water either."

"You like it better than Rudy does." Mom hurls the scrubber at me. "I'll pay you a dollar."

"Two dollars," I say.

"A dollar fifty."

"Dollar seventy-five."

"Dollar sixty-two."

"Okay, okay, I'll do it."

It's actually pretty easy to clean Einstein's aquarium. The difficult part is not bumping Einstein with the scrubber. He's active today, wriggling back and forth. It's like he's asking me question after question. When are we moving? Where are we going? You're not going to forget to pack my food, are you? Why are your pants all puckered?

"They're here!" Mom calls out. "Hide!"

Rudy and I scramble up onto his bedroom-closet shelf. It's a place we often hang out in. We've got two flashlights, a deck of cards and even some leftover tortilla chips stashed away. The tortilla chips taste a little like wet dust, but we eat them anyway. We play War, then make up a game called Peace. It's not the most exciting game. When the bedroom door cracks open, we stop playing and sit very still. I gesture to Rudy to hold his breath.

Clip clip clippity. Someone wearing high heels enters the room. "This would be a marvelous room for my office," she says.

A man answers, "Hmmm."

"We'd have to change the ceiling light though."

"Tacky," the man mutters.

"You can say that again."

"Tacky."

Clip clip clippity. Clump clump clump. The two walk across the bedroom floor. "We'd give these windows a wash too," the woman says.

"Filthy," the man says.

"You can say that again."

"Filthy."

At this point, Rudy decides it's a great time to scratch his head. As he lifts his hand in the dark, his elbow bashes my lip. My mouth goes numb and fattens like a marshmallow swelling over a fire. As I wince from the pain, the closet shelf creaks beneath me.

"Did you hear that?" the man asks.

"Hear what?"

"In the closet. Rats."

"You're always hearing things, Arnold."

Rats. Good idea. I draw my fingernails against the shelf. *Scritch scratch scritch.*

"What about that?" the man squeaks.

"What about what?"

I draw my nails along the shelf again, this time more loudly. *SCRITCH SCRATCH SCRITCH.*

"Now *that* I heard," the woman says.

"There's rats in this house, Alissa. Hundreds, I bet! Giant rats with long teeth and disgusting pink tails."

"What's *that?*" the woman asks. She has clearly seen something she doesn't like.

"It's…a potato! It looks like it has been gnawed on by the rats!"

"We've got to get out of here, Arnold. Immediately. Quick, out that dirty window."

Rudy and I listen as the two clamber through Rudy's bedroom window and crash into the hydrangea bush below.

Rudy and I unfold ourselves from the closet, laughing so hard we can barely catch our breath. We watch the couple get into their car and start the engine. Martian Planet runs to the front door and starts chasing them down the road. "Hey! Where are you going?" She dives into an electric car and tears off in hot pursuit.

As soon as she's out of sight, a big dirty F-350 pickup truck drives up. Dad!

I always forget how enormous my father is. He makes Popeye look puny. He's wearing his plaid shirt with the sleeves torn off. He still has his work boots on, but within two hours he'll be wearing his pink fluffy slippers. Mom got them for him as a joke, but he loves them.

"Hey!" Dad opens his arms wide, and I swear the lawn shrinks.

"Dad! Your lip." Rudy touches Dad's mouth.

Dad has a fat lip just like I do!

"Did a tree fall on you?" I ask.

"No, nothing like that," Dad says, shaking his head. "You won't believe it. We were having a surprise birthday party for one of the guys in camp. Three of us were hiding in the closet. Then one of the guys decides to scratch his head and I get an elbow in the mouth!"

"I believe that," I say.

"What happened to *your* lip?" Dad asks.

"A tree fell on me."

Dad laughs. "Ice cream?"

"Yeah!"

As we always do when Dad gets home, we walk down to the Scoop. Rudy rides on Dad's left shoulder and I ride on Dad's right. Sure, Mom says we get it from our great-grandmother. But I'll bet that riding on Dad's shoulders is the real reason Rudy and I like to be up high.

Chapter Seven

"Goodnight!" I yell, and turn off my light.

The alarm clock under my pillow digs into the back of my head. The pillow will muffle the bell when it rings at 2:00 AM. And Dad's snores will muffle my footsteps.

I fall asleep to the clock's faint *tick-tick-tick* through the feathers. I have a nightmare about a woman in high heels prying the walls off our house. It's a relief when the alarm goes off and wakes me. I shuffle into my slippers and quietly open my bedroom door. Dad's snores rumble through the house. It's like he's got logging machinery in his throat.

I unlock the front door and step onto the porch. This is too easy! I head straight for Martian Planet's toothy face. I give the sign a yank. It slides out of the ground, heavier than I imagined. I lug it to the back of the house and hide it under the back stairs. Piece of cake!

Then something moves in the dark. A pair of eyes gleam in the night. A raccoon? Or something scarier? As I run, my ankle brushes against the beast's fur. I'm pretty sure it swats at me with its long claws as I fly into the house. I'm lucky to be alive!

I curl up under the covers with my heart pounding. But I'm happy. After all, our house is officially *not* for sale!

★　★　★

I wake up to the whistle of the kettle, and I lie in bed listening to Mom and Dad murmuring in the kitchen. Every so often, they burst into laughter.

Eventually, Rudy's door creaks open and I hear him pad into the kitchen, yawning.

"Here's my big boy!" Dad says. "Let's see how much you've grown."

The Taller Cupboard door whines on its hinges. The inside of the door is covered in pencil marks. *Rudy, 3 years old. Cyrus, 7.*

"Are you on your tiptoes?" Dad asks.

"Stop trying to squish me!"

I know Dad is pushing on Rudy's head, accusing him of cheating. He always does that. And I know Mom is watching from the kitchen couch, drinking coffee from her green mug with the broken handle. I'll go down any minute and get measured too. But for now, I'm cozy, listening to the music of my family's voices.

"You've grown an inch in two months! What has your mom been feeding you?"

"Kumquats and quinoa."

Then it happens. Mom notices. "The For Sale sign is gone!"

I hear Rudy run to the window. "Does that mean we've sold the house?" he asks.

I put on my slippers and try to saunter casually into the kitchen.

"What kind of person goes around stealing For Sale signs?" Mom asks.

"A For Sale-sign stealer?" I suggest.

Mom gets on the phone. "Marsha? Some thief stole our sign. Yes, I need another one."

Rudy looks freaked out. "We had a thief? In our yard? While we were sleeping?"

"Breathe, Rudy," Dad says.

"Yeah, Rudy." I wink at him. "Looks like some *rat* came and took our For Sale sign."

I put my finger to my lips when Mom and Dad aren't looking. Rudy's eyes go wide.

Chapter Eight

"Rudy" finds me in the change room before gymnastics. He pulls out a fancy, old-fashioned-looking piece of paper from his backpack.

"How did you know my full name wasn't Rudy James Walker?" he asks me.

I hold the birth certificate to the light, make a big deal of inspecting it. Sure enough, the boy isn't Rudy James Walker. He's Rudyard James Walker.

"Wow. You were born in Kamsack, Saskatchewan?"

"I don't know. I was born in a hospital."

"In 1946?"

Rudy shrugs. "Maybe?"

"I don't think this is your birth certificate. Could it be your dad's?"

"It's probably Grandpa's. He lives with us."

"Don't you know your grandfather's name?"

"Yeah. It's Grandpa."

"Right."

"My name is Rudy. I swear!"

"Okay," I say. "I believe you."

I don't, really. But the world sure doesn't need another anxious Rudy.

★ ★ ★

When I get home from gymnastics, there's a new sign in the yard. Good as new. When no one's looking, I give it a push. It's loose enough.

At bedtime, I set the alarm clock. At two in the morning, I tiptoe out of the house and pull the second sign out of the ground. I tuck it under the back stairs

with the first one. Then I run as fast as I can back into the house, avoiding sharp-toothed raccoons, hungry coyotes and a blood-thirsty lynx. I fall asleep again to the sound of my thudding heart.

"The rat hit again," Rudy tells Mom in the morning. He winks at me.

Mom slams her green mug down. Coffee splashes everywhere. Mom gets on the phone. "We need ten this time," she tells Martian Planet. "You heard me. Ten."

Martian Planet's at the house in no time with a forest of For Sale signs. Mom and Dad hammer each one deep into the ground with sledgehammers.

When they're done, Dad gives each sign a little tug. "Nice and tight," he says.

It's raining when I sneak out after midnight. It takes forever to pull all of the signs out of the lawn. They're slippery. I stack them under the back stairs while black bears and wolverines sniff at my ankles. Finally, I climb back into bed, soaking and muddy, my hands raw with slivers.

"Some practical joker," Mom is muttering when I wake up. "Maybe that group Anonymous that hacks into websites."

"I don't think so," Dad says. He raises his voice. "I think it's closer to home. Maybe these muddy size-5 slipper prints in the hallway have something to do with it. And look, they lead right to this bedroom door."

Uh-oh.

"CYRUS!!!!!!!!!"

I leap out of bed, getting tangled in my sheets. I fall onto my Battle of Helm's Deep LEGO set and whimper as its thirteen hundred pieces scatter.

I stumble into the hallway. "Y-y-y-yes?"

"Really, Cyrus?" Mom says.

Dad hands me the sledgehammer. "Put them back."

"Why did you do it?" Mom asks.

My heart lurches. "Isn't it obvious? I don't want to move! I don't want to be—nowhere!"

I run back into my room. I burrow under my covers. My stomach hurts, and I can't catch my breath. I feel angry and ashamed, but mostly I feel frightened.

Mom comes into my room. "Sweetheart…"

I don't answer.

"Cyrus, breathe. Take deep breaths. Like this."

Mom starts drawing long, slow breaths, like she's done a hundred times with Rudy.

It's hard at first, but I take a few long swallows of air. "Is this what Rudy feels like?" I ask. My voice is trembling.

"Yep."

"It's awful."

"It sure is."

"Rudy is pretty brave to go through this all the time. A brave wolf."

Mom smiles. "Are you ready to talk now?"

"I had a nightmare last night," I say. "You, Dad and Rudy were in a new house and I was outside, crawling past like a baby. You were all happy and celebrating. You didn't even see me."

"Oh, Cyrus," Mom says. She kneels beside my bed. "That's just a nightmare. That would never really happen."

"But when I was a baby, I had to find you and Dad. You didn't even know that I existed. I don't really have Great-Grandma's trapeze genes—not like Rudy does."

"We found you too, honey. You might not have Great-Grandma's genes, but as soon as I laid eyes on you, I knew you were my son. And—don't forget this—I knew that I was your mother."

I start to cry. But it feels nice, like a warm rain.

"Listen. I'll tell you what. On moving day, when we drive to our new house, I'll hold your hand the whole way. I won't let go, okay?"

"Promise?"

"Promise."

Mom smiles and squeezes me. Everything starts to feel normal again. I can't believe that I was so frightened.

Chapter Nine

"The new owners won't miss this," Mom says. She has removed the screws from the Taller Cupboard hinges and is hoisting the door onto her shoulder.

Everything is in the moving van, including Einstein, who splashes around in a mason jar. Dad is trying to talk Rudy down from the top of the moving van, where he's been sobbing for an hour.

"Take your last breath of urban air," Mom says, shoving the Taller Cupboard door into the back of the van. "Soon your nostrils will fill with the marvelous aroma of manure."

We didn't have to get a smaller house after all.

Mom and Dad bought a farmhouse in the country, with a pond and a barn filled with real rats.

"Come on, Rudy," I call up. "Let's go see the cows!"

"No."

"They're pretty cows."

"No!"

"Wait, I know!"

I run into our empty house. My steps echo as I enter my old bedroom. I feel around on the top shelf of my closet. Sure enough, I find our old stash. A pile of potatoes with holes drilled into them. I run back outside.

"Look, Rudy. We'll take these with us."

Rudy looks at the potatoes in my hands. He smiles.

"It'll feel like home in no time," I tell him.

Once we're all in the van, Mom reaches for my hand and squeezes. I squeeze back.

At a red light a block from home, a car pulls up beside us. The driver is gesturing wildly at us.

He rolls down his window. "There's a cat!" he yells. "On the roof of your van!"

As Rudy helps Dad rescue Wigglechin, Mom and I stay in the van, holding hands. We hold hands all the way to the new house. Except once. Just to see if I'll go hurtling into space, I let go for half a second. But I stay right where I am, hurtling down the highway with my family.

Sara Cassidy has worked as a youth-hostel manager, a newspaper reporter and a tree planter in five Canadian provinces. Her poetry, fiction and articles have been widely published, and she has won a Gold National Magazine Award. She lives in Victoria, British Columbia, with her three children. For more information, visit www.saracassidywriter.com.

Orca Echoes

Orca Echoes

Orca Echoes

Orca Echoes

Prospect Heights Public Library
12 N. Elm Street
Prospect Heights, IL 60070
www.phpl.info